MILLIE'S WAR

By

Dorian Mode

FOR ALL ENQUIRIES CONTACT: ORiGiN™ Theatrical
PO BOX Q1235, QVB Post Office, Sydney, NSW, 1230, Australia
Phone: (61 2) 8514 5201 Fax (61 2) 9299 2920
enquiries@originmusic.com.au   www.origintheatrical.com.au
Part of the ORiGiN™ Music Group
An Australian Independent Music Company

IMPORTANT NOTICE

First Published © 2018 ORiGiN™ Theatrical

The amateur and professional acting rights to this work are controlled exclusively by ORiGiN™ Theatrical (the publisher). Permission in writing is required by ORiGiN™ Theatrical, or their agent, before a performance is given. A performance is given any time it is acted before an audience. A royalty fee is payable before each and every performance regardless of whether it is for a non-profit organisation or if an admission is charged.

The publication of this play does not mean that the amateur and professional performance rights are available. It is highly recommended that you apply for performance rights before starting rehearsals and/or booking rehearsal or performance spaces.

Visit the ORiGiN™ Theatrical website for applications and information www.origintheatrical.com.au or address your inquiry to ORiGiN™ Theatrical, PO Box Q1235, QVB Post Office, Sydney, NSW 1230, Australia.

This work is fully protected by copyright. No alterations, substitutions or deletions can be made to this work without the prior consent of the publisher. It is expressly prohibited to broadcast, televise, film, videotape, record, translate or transmit to subscribers through a diffusion service that currently exists or is yet to be invented, this work or any portion thereof whatsoever without permission in writing from the publisher.

Copying or reproducing, without permission, of all or any part of this book, in any form, is an infringement of copyright. Copyright provides the creators with an incentive to invest their time, talent and other resources to create new works. Authors earn their living from the royalties they receive from book sales and from the performance of the work. Copyright law provides a legal framework for control of their creations.

Whenever this play is produced, the billing and credit requirements *must* appear on all programs distributed in connection with the performance and in all instances in which the title of the play appears for the purposes of advertising, seeking publicity for the play or otherwise exploiting the play and/or a performance(s).

While this play may contain references to brand names or trademarks owned by third parties, or make reference to public figures, ORiGiN™ Theatrical should not be considered to be necessarily endorsing or otherwise attempting to promote an affiliation with any of the owners of the brand names or trademarks or public figures. Such references are solely for use in a dramatic context.

LANGUAGE NOTE

Licensees are welcome to make small alterations to the language that is used is this play so as to make it suitable for a younger cast and/or audience.

MUSIC USE NOTE

Licensees are solely responsible for obtaining formal written permission from copyright owners to use copyrighted music in the performance of this play and are strongly cautioned to do so. If no such permission is obtained by the licensee, then the licensee must use only original music that the licensee owns and controls. Licensees are solely responsible and liable for all music clearances and shall indemnify the copyright owners of the play(s) and their licensing agent, ORiGiN™ Theatrical, against any costs, expenses, losses and liabilities arising from the use of music by licensees. Please contact the appropriate music licensing authority in your territory for the rights to any incidental music. In Australia and New Zealand, contact APRA AMCOS apraamcos.com.au.

If you are in any doubt about any of the above then contact ORiGiN™ Theatrical.

For complete listing of plays and musicals available to perform and all licence enquiries, contact ORiGiN™ Theatrical.

---

www.origintheatrical.com.au
+ 61 2 8514 5201

AND HERE ARE THE RULES IN PLAIN ENGLISH FOR YOU...

DO NOT perform this play without getting permission from ORiGiN™ Theatrical first. In 99% of cases you'll need to pay us money to be allowed to stage a performance. This money goes to the author(s) of the show who shed blood, sweat and tears creating this play. Please don't rob them of their livelihood.
Go online www.origintheatrical.com.au or call +61 2 8514 5201

DO NOT make a copy of this book by photocopying, scanning, taking a photo, retyping (on a computer or a typewriter), or using a pencil, pen or chalkboard. If you want to purchase more copies contact ORiGiN™ Theatrical.
Go online www.origintheatrical.com.au or call +61 2 8514 5201

DO NOT make any changes to the text without first getting permission from ORiGiN™ Theatrical in writing. Sometimes you'll be allowed to make changes and sometimes you won't. Please always check with us first.
Go online www.origintheatrical.com.au or call +61 2 8514 5201

DO NOT record your performances or rehearsals in anyway without first getting permission from ORiGiN™ Theatrical. We know everyone wants to try and record everything on their phones these days. We get it. But please don't encourage them or give them permission. Sometimes there are important contractual reasons as to why we can't give you permission to record it. And sometimes there aren't any reasons and we can say YES. Please just check with us first.
Go online www.origintheatrical.com.au or call +61 2 8514 5201

DO contract ORiGiN™ Theatrical if you have any questions about anything. At all. And we mean anything. One of us that works here (not me) has a peculiar interest in recording the unusual bird calls of the adult hoatzin (a species of tropical bird found in wet forest and mangrove of the Amazon and the Orinoco delta in South America) so we should be able to answer any questions you have about the Hoatzin. Plus we know some things about some other things too.

Thank you for taking the time to read this.

ABOUT THE AUTHOR

Dorian Mode is the author of the novels Café in Venice (Penguin) and Mozart Maulers (Penguin). He's written for The Age, Sydney Morning Herald and leading magazines and was the back-page columnist for The Australian Writer's Guild Magazine. His plays are published in Australia and the UK.

He has won several university scholarships and holds a Master's Degree and Doctorate and lectured in creative writing at Newcastle University.

FOR SHERYL

CAST

ALF
President of the RSL Club, 60's. Tweed jacket, regimental tie, highly polished shoes, walking stick, sprig of rosemary in the lapel. RSL Club badge.

MORRIS
Club Treasurer, 60's, hearing aid. cardigan, beret, sprig of rosemary in the lapel. RSL Club badge.

PERCY
Club Secretary, 60's. Navy blue squadron jacket, cravat, thin moustache, sprig of rosemary in the lapel. RSL Club badge.

KEVIN
Junior Board member. Mid 40's, overly tanned. Hawaiian-Shirt. Ray-Bans. RSL Club badge.

MILLIE
20's, pregnant, 80's power suits, corn chip earrings, padded shoulders. Big hair.

ROSEMARY
30's, short cropped punk hair. Dressed like an English Professor in sneakers.

BEV
40's. Chain smoker. Short skirt. Push-up bra. Tobacco chuckle.

PUNTER/SALVO/BRIAN (V.O.) (if required, played by stagehand)

2 females, 4 males, plus stage-hand walk-ons where required.

Photos: The Australian War Memorial

Photos: The Australian War Memorial

SETTING: Returned Servicemen's Club (RSL) in regional Australia

TIME: 1980 something

ACT 1 SCENE 1

In the dark we hear 'God Save The Queen' by The Sex Pistols.

A spotlight is raised on a PORTRAIT OF A YOUNG QUEEN ELIZABETH in the back corner Stage Left.

As the punk rock soundscape fades, lights are raised. Our punk music melds with the dulcet tones of Dame Vera Lynn warbling 'The White Cliffs of Dover'. Soon Dame Vera fades and we hear the saccharine melodies of poker machines.

We hear an announcement: "number 15, yer pie and chips is ready to be collected from the bar."

Front Stage Right we see a round table set with four coasters.

Stage Left, BEV is cleaning glasses at the bar. A serving of pie and chips sits on the bar congealing. Our yawning barmaid furtively steals an occasional chip from the plate. PUNTER collects the meal and exits the stage.

In a far corner we see a twinkling Christmas Tree draped with yuletide decorations.

Stage Right back we see a row of poker machines. Occasionally, throughout the performance, Punter wanders onto stage in the background with a beer or cigarette to play the machines in the shadows.

Front Stage Left we see a horizontal glass cabinet filled with war memorabilia. A spotlight illuminates its centrepiece: a flag with the Japanese Rising Sun.

ALF, MORRIS, PERCY and KEVIN enter and sit at the table.

We suddenly hear an announcement over the intercom.

BRIAN (V.O.)
Attention patrons...

>A plastic Legacy-style torch lights in the corner of the stage.

BRIAN (V.O.)
Will you please be upstanding for the ode.

>The quartet of old soldiers silently stand, turn and face west.

BRIAN (V.O.)
"They shall grow not old, as we that are left grow old;
Age shall not weary them, nor the years condemn.
At the going down of the sun and in the morning
We will remember them. Lest we forget."

CAST
Lest we forget...

>We hear the LAST POST.

BRIAN (V.O.)
Thank you patrons.

>Lights are raised over the table. Kevin picks at a ukulele (quietly enough not to distract the dialogue).
>
>Morris stands to read a note.

The soundtrack of the poker machines fades.

He clears his throat. This takes long enough for comic effect.

Alf, the Club President, irritably looks at his watch as the man continues to clear his throat: an small opera in phlegm.

He finally speaks.

MORRIS
(Clearing his throat, reading)
Sorry, gentlemen I've been eating a lot of cheese lately. Always risky. Had the plumber out twice this month to unblock the toilet. My Ivy loves French cheeses, you see. But too much phlegm. No wonder the Frogs surrendered in 1940. You can't win a war with cheese.

KEVIN
You might be lactose intolerant.

PERCY
My Doris has that. Sprinkled Parmesan cheese on her Lasagne once and she blew her dentures clean across the floor.

MORRIS
Really?

PERCY
Wouldn't have minded but we were dining at that revolving restaurant in that new Centrepoint Tower.

KEVIN
Centrepoint. Ahh, the great wastepaper basket in the sky.

        Alf irritably looks at his watch.

MORRIS
My Ivy's keen to pop up and take a look. The restaurant's revolting, you say...?

PERCY
Revolving.

        Morris adjusts his hearing aid.

MORRIS
Revolving? Oh dear. That won't do. I don't like heights. It's all right for you. You were a bomber pilot in the war.

PERCY
Just don't look down. That's what I used to tell the new boys.

KEVIN
I didn't know Doris wore dentures.

PERCY
Yes. Since '43. Had her remaining teeth knocked out for our wedding. So she could be fitted for dentures. People did that then. Cosmetic dentistry they call it now. But that's how we found out she was lactose intolerant.

KEVIN
Reckon I'm lactose intolerant. Every time I-

ALF
(Jumping to his feet)

I tell you something for nothing! I'm bloody 'you lot' intolerant. Get on with proceedings, Mr Treasurer! (sotto voce) Strike me pink!

Alf sits.

MORRIS
Sorry, Alf. Right you are.

He clears his throat.

ALF
And don't start that again. Get on with it, man.

MORRIS
Right you are.

ALF
And tell me. Why aren't we in the damn boardroom? Why are we stuck out here in the club.

MORRIS
Conference. Brian makes extra money for the club by letting out the boardroom to business groups. This one's a franchisees conference, I believe. Doggy Doo Dahs.

ALF
What?

MORRIS
It's a mobile dog grooming service.

Off stage we hear chanting:
I feel great! Woof woof woof!
I'm a winner! Woof woof woof!

KEVIN
Centrepoint. Ahh, the great wastepaper basket in the sky.

>   Alf irritably looks at his watch.

MORRIS
My Ivy's keen to pop up and take a look. The restaurant's revolting, you say...?

PERCY
Revolving.

>   Morris adjusts his hearing aid.

MORRIS
Revolving? Oh dear. That won't do. I don't like heights. It's all right for you. You were a bomber pilot in the war.

PERCY
Just don't look down. That's what I used to tell the new boys.

KEVIN
I didn't know Doris wore dentures.

PERCY
Yes. Since '43. Had her remaining teeth knocked out for our wedding. So she could be fitted for dentures. People did that then. Cosmetic dentistry they call it now. But that's how we found out she was lactose intolerant.

KEVIN
Reckon I'm lactose intolerant. Every time I-

ALF
(Jumping to his feet)

I tell you something for nothing! I'm bloody 'you lot' intolerant. Get on with proceedings, Mr Treasurer! (sotto voce) Strike me pink!

>Alf sits.

MORRIS
Sorry, Alf. Right you are.

>He clears his throat.

ALF
And don't start that again. Get on with it, man.

MORRIS
Right you are.

ALF
And tell me. Why aren't we in the damn boardroom? Why are we stuck out here in the club.

MORRIS
Conference. Brian makes extra money for the club by letting out the boardroom to business groups. This one's a franchisees conference, I believe. Doggy Doo Dahs.

ALF
What?

MORRIS
It's a mobile dog grooming service.

>Off stage we hear chanting:
>*I feel great! Woof woof woof!*
>*I'm a winner! Woof woof woof!*

ALF
Bloody disgrace! The boardroom is for the *board*!

MORRIS
Fair point, well made. Now, then. (reading) Absent from this evening's meeting, Mr Spencer Crombie. (to Alf) He's got trouble with his boils again. Absent Mr Jack Davis DFC - he's had a stroke and would be here but for dribbling down his shirt whenever he hears the sound of running water.

PERCY
(nodding)
Old Nev's had a stroke, too.

MORRIS
Who?

PERCY
You know. Old Neville Primrose. Flew Kittyhawks in North Africa. Played bowls with us that day when Darcy had trouble with his veins.

> Alf irritably taps his watch at Morris.

MORRIS
(to Alf)
Yes, yes, of course. Sorry Alf. (reading) Absent Mr Gilbert Nuttle - (to Alf) - the bus doesn't pass his retirement village, anymore. He's written to the council about it. No reply. (to Percy) I formally ask the club secretary to make a note of that. Can I have someone second that?

KEVIN
(lazily raises hand)

Second.

MORRIS
Can you make a note of that please, Percy?

                            Percy scribbles in a note book.

Absent Mr Charlie Dawkins. He's had a triple bypass. Absent Mr-

ALF
Christ on bike! It's like the land of the living dead.

MORRIS
-absent Mr Tobias Cruickshank. Old Toby said he would be here but he's suffering with a lot of chaffing in the...Netherlands-

PERCY
Holland?

MORRIS
(pointing at his crotch)
The low countries.

ALF
(irritably, to himself)
Fat lot of use he would have been in the jungle fighting, Tojo. Bloody chaffing!

MORRIS
(tapping hearing aid)
Toejam? That can happen in the tropics.

ALF
(fuming)

Look, can we have the absentee list *without* the usual medical reports, Mr Treasurer?

> Bev - wearing a Santa Hat - sets four beers on the table. She drapes her impressive udders over Kevin.

BEV
There you are gentlemen. Courtesy of the management. Brian says sorry about the boardroom. We don't have a designated conference room yet. It's on the agenda but. Are yous okay out here in the bar?

KEVIN
Be happier if you sat on my lap, Bev.

BEV
(winking at Kevin)
Play yer cards, right, Sweetie and Santa will bring yer something special for Christmas.

PERCY
Yes, we're quite alright, luvvy. Thank Brian for us.

ALF
No we're not bloody alright! How dare Brian stick us out here for our monthly board meeting. Bloody disgrace. This club was built on the bodies of our former comrades.

KEVIN
(soto voce)
And here I was thinking it was built on a disused swamp.

BEV
Do you want me to fetch, Brian, Alf?

ALF
No. I'm already late. But I want it known that I'm not happy about this. Free drinks or no free drinks! The boardroom is just that: for the *board*.

> Bev shrugs and leaves.

MORRIS
(indicating cast)
So to proceedings. Those present: Club Treasurer, Mr Morris Klein. Junior Board Member Mr Kevin O'Connell. Club Secretary Mr Percival Scott DFC and the honourable Club President Mr Alfred Watson A.M. O.B.E. M.M-

ALF
Yes. Yes. Yes. We don't need all the gongs every time, Morris. Let's just get on with it, shall we? I'm meeting my granddaughter for Chinese after this board meeting.

KEVIN
(singing, Python style)
I like Chinese....I like Chinese...

ALF
Shut up, fool!

> Kevin shrugs and removes his Ray-Bans

MORRIS
You can't speak to Kevin like that, Alf. We need to respect our junior members. They're the future of the club.

Kevin was at Long Tan.

ALF
'Fake Tan' more like it.

MORRIS
No, not heard of that one. Is that in Vietnam? No, he was definitely at Long Tan. Weren't you Kevin? Tell him. Go on.

>   Kevin shrugs.

KEVIN
(thinking)
I was either in the Battle of Long Tan... or in a whore house in Saigon shagging a lass named Curly Shirley. She was a Saigon whore with a perm. That I *do* remember. The things that girl could do. You see, I was on these magic mushrooms at the time and-

MORRIS
But you were in D Company. Gary remembers you at the Bren Gun that day. Firing into the rubber plantation.

KEVIN
(thinking)
I do recall a lot of rubber...

MORRIS
(nodding to the others)
See!

KEVIN
(thinking)
Or was it 'rubbers'...?

ALF
If he's the future, God save us.

> Kevin nods, pensively, still in thought.

MORRIS
That segues rather neatly into this new business.

ALF
What *new* business?

MORRIS
Women in war.

ALF
What bloody women in war?

MORRIS
A group of young women asked to join our ANZAC Day march next year.

ALF
Nurses?

MORRIS
Not exactly.

ALF
WAAFS?

MORRIS
Eh...not exactly.

ALF
Who are these women, then?

MORRIS
Feminists.

ALF
Feminists?

MORRIS
(nodding)
Feminists.

ALF
What do bloody feminists want with our march?

MORRIS
Say what?

ALF
What do they want, Morris?

MORRIS
(tapping his hearing aid)
What?

ALF
Turn up that *bloody* gramophone in your ear, Morris. What do they *want*, man?

MORRIS
Oh. I see. They wish to march to remember women raped in war.

                        Alf stands to his feet and points his walking stick at Morris.

ALF
Over my dead body.

>Bev returns from the bar with a bowl of peanuts.

BEV
Necrophilia

ALF
What?

KEVIN
The rape of dead bodies. Necrophilia.

>Kevin pulls out a ukulele and improvises a song.

KEVIN
(singing/playing joyfully)
Her name was Maisie.
I thought her lazy.
But when I wooed her,
And later screwed her,
We never spoke again.
She was a corpse.

ALF
Must you insist on bringing that bloody toy guitar everywhere you go?

KEVIN
Part of my therapy. My shrink said to manifest my demons through song.

BEV
Worked for Barry Manilow.

ALF
Why is it that so many of your lot came back psychotic? We saw much more action than your lot did. We coped. We got on with our lives without playing a tiny guitar and smoking marry-a-jew-arna.

KEVIN
Perhaps you repressed it.

ALF
(Gets to his feet)
Repressed it? *Repressed it?* Of course we bloody repressed it. We had a nation to build.

MORRIS
I think they came back a little damaged because the public shunned them, Alf.

      Alf sits and sighs.

PERCY
True. They didn't have grand parades through the city like we did, Alf, if you remember.

MORRIS
That's right. Our fighting was for the greater good. To stop fascism. That's why I fought.

ALF
Fought!? You were a cook in the bloody desert. You mostly fought the Italians for chicken recipes.

25

BEV
God! That reminds me. Me chicken pies!

Bev rushes offstage.

MORRIS
(reflects, eyes glazed in memory)
True. What the Italians could do with a tomato and a little oregano would make a sergeant of the mess weep.

ALF
Listen, you lot! I'm not having a gang of lesbians-

KEVIN
Feminists.

ALF
What did I say?

KEVIN
Lesbians.

PERCY
I heard him say lesbians.

MORRIS
I thought he said Libyans. I distinctly remember talking about chicken recipes in Libya. (to Kevin) I was stationed there in the war, you know. Now, the Italians could take some rice, a tomato and a stick of-

ALF
Morris! Can we please stick to the agenda for once.

Kevin strums a chord and sings.

KEVIN
(singing/playing)
Agenda!
A mind bender!
Never meant to offend her.
But I had my agenda.
So I dropped my pants.

ALF
Listen, fool. I'll shove that thing where the sun don't shine-

KEVIN
Melbourne?

PERCY
My niece lives in Melbourne.

KEVIN
They all wear black in Melbourne. I'm told it's to absorb the sun. Me? I love the sun.

>Kevin removes his shirt and indicates his tan.
>
>Alf is apoplectic with rage.

ALF
For the love of Mike! Put your bloody shirt back on, idiot. This is not a resort. (Turns to Morris and Percy) And you two. Every time we have a meeting we get off bloody topic and the damn thing ends up going for hours. I'm meeting my granddaughter for Chinese.

KEVIN
(singing)

I like Chinese....

> Bev comes over with a plate of party pies.

BEV
Barry apologises for the inconvenience and would like yous all to have dinner on us.

ALF
This is what he calls *dinner?* Luke-warm pies?

BEV
It beats 'shit on a shingle', Alf. Do you want 'em or not? Otherwise I'll take 'em home for me tea.

ALF
We don't want them. Take them away.

> Kevin and Morris snatch a pie.
>
> Bev exits the stage with the pies.

ALF
(over his shoulder)
And you can tell Brian to stick them where the sun don't shine!

KEVIN
Melbourne?

> Bev returns with a bouquet of flowers and then exits the stage.

ALF
So now Brian's buying us flowers?

PERCY
No. These are from me. I thought the ladies might appreciate it. They're coming in to meet us to talk about joining the march. I see you're wearing a tie today. Good show.

KEVIN
Alf wears a tie to the beach.

ALF
I'm wearing a tie because I'm meeting my granddaughter. Listen, forget the flowers.

MORRIS
Ladies like flowers.

ALF
Ladies? If we're meeting a group of bloody feminists, they don't want flowers. They want...bloody overalls.

KEVIN
For painting?

MORRIS
(adjusting his hearing aid)
Someone said they're painting the boardroom today?

PERCY
They might be.

ALF
Listen you dribbling fools-

PERCY
Listen! Don't come all 'Captain Chocko Watson' with us. You're not an officer anymore. You're a retired accountant.

KEVIN
Yeah, you can only boss people around at the end of the fiscal year.

> Bev returns with more flowers and a box of chocolates.

ALF
How many flowers did you buy, Percy? We'll be overrun by bees, next. Take all these flowers away.

MORRIS
Bees! That's reminds me. My Ivy said to ask. Are beehives tax-deductible?

BEV
(cleaning an ashtray)
Very popular in the late 60s. With the girl groups. Used to have one meself. Looked like Dusty Springfield only with bigger knockers. (She winks a curtain of eyelash at Kevin)

MORRIS
No...honey bees, I mean. Excellent for the garden.

ALF
Listen you two, idiots. During the war I had 46 men under me-

KEVIN
Kinky.

> Alf pins him with a look before addressing the men.
>
> Bev removes the flowers and sets them over on the bar.

ALF
-and any one of 'em had more brains than you lot put together.

> Alf takes a gulp of beer and takes a deep breath. He settles himself.
>
> Suddenly one of the 'stagehands' at the pokies wanders over an interrupts them holding a $10 note.

PUNTER
(thrusting a $10 note)
Have any of yous got change for ten bucks?

ALF
Can't you see we're in a board meeting? Get lost.

PUNTER
Can yous at least mind me machine while I get change?

ALF
No. Take a hike, chum.

> The boozy punter shrugs before staggering off-stage.

ALF
This is why we need the bloody boardroom!

> Off stage we hear (stagehands) chanting *I feel great woof woof woof. I'm a winner woof woof woof.*

Alf throws his hands in the air.

PERCY
Why are you so cranky today, Alf?

ALF
(quietly)
Don't you understand? These women are man-haters. They despise people like us. They come here to bring shame on our day. To dishonour the graves of our comrades. And here you are buying them *flowers!* Next you'll be buying them bloody *chocolates!*

Behind Alf's back, Kevin frisbees the box of chocolates to Bev at the bar.

MILLIE and ROSEMARY enter. Alf has his back to them at the table and doesn't immediately see them.

Millie is pregnant and beginning to show.

Morris and Percy stand for the young ladies. Kevin sits, picking at his uke, until nudged by one of the older gentleman to stand for the ladies.

ALF
Bloody flowers. I'm telling you. These women-

> Alf notices his comrades standing. He suddenly looks over his shoulder to see two women before him.
>
> Alf rushes over and kisses Millie on the cheek.

ALF
Oh hello Millie, luv. (to Kevin) Kevin, I don't think you've met my granddaughter Millie and this is Miss...?

MILLIE
This is my friend Dr. Rosemary Smith. Dr Smith teaches modern history at my university.

> They shake hands.

ALF
You're early, luvvy. I'm sorry to be rude but Poppy's a little busy right now. You see, we're meeting some lesbians.

KEVIN
Feminists.

MORRIS
(adjusting his hearing aid)
Libyans.

ALF
For the final time, Morris, these women are not Libyans. This has nothing to do with Libya!

> Kevin plays and sings in the style of Groucho Marx. (Sung to

the tune of 'Lydia the Tattooed Lady'.)

KEVIN
(singing/playing)
Oh Libya,
Oh Libya,
Oh have you seen Libya?
Oh Libya the oil rich country,
It's a riot,
You'll be laughing,
Swing on over,
Meet Gaddafi.

ALF
You can put that bloody guitar away. We have a serious meeting with these feminists.

KEVIN
(to the girls)
Thought it might help. Healing power of song. Stopped the Vietnam War, you know.

ROSEMARY
(smiling)
That and thousands of protestors.

ALF
Oh, don't agree with him, luv. You'll never shut him up. Not right in the head. Ever since the 'fake tan' incident.

MORRIS
(frowning at Alf)
Kevin was in Vietnam.

ROSEMARY
You were in Nam? What year?

KEVIN
Can't remember.

> Rosemary looks puzzled.

ROSEMARY
You must have seen some shocking things.

KEVIN
True. There was this lass, Curly Shirley. Now what she could do with a ping-pong ball and a-

ALF
Ladies present!

PERCY
Now the introductions are over I think we should get started. Do you mind if I take notes, ladies. I'm the club secretary. We don't have access to the boardroom tonight. We've been passed over for a Dog Grooming Conference. They're running over time. Brian thought they'd be finished by now. Millie, I think you know our club treasurer Mr-

> Alf stands, mouth agape.

ALF
(throws out his hands)
Hang on! Hang on!! What do you mean get started? What are you banging on about?

> Bev comes over with a plate of mini sausage rolls.

BEV
Here you are, gentlemen. Courtesy of the management. Brian has also offered to give each board member $10 worth of free raffle tickets for the inconvenience.

PERCY
Thought you knew, Alf. Didn't Millie tell you?

                    Percy looks at Millie and shrugs.

MILLIE
(grimacing)
Eh...never quite found the right moment.

PERCY
These are the ladies representing the group who wish to march with us.

                    Alf is stunned to silence.

KEVIN
It's true, Alf. Purce told me at the bar.

ALF
Milliscent! You're not mixed up with this lesbian business.

KEVIN
Feminist.

MORRIS
(tapping hearing aid)
Libyan.

KEVIN
(singin/playing)

Oh...Lybia, oh Lybia...oh....

> Alf pokes Kevin's ukulele with his walking stick so he can't play it.

MILLIE
Pop, we are not lesbians, feminists or Libyans (shrugs at Rosemary). We're simply young women who want to remember women who suffered in war.

ROSEMARY
Women raped in war. Women murdered in war. Women abused by men.

ALF
All hail the Female Eunuch!

MILLIE
Pop we've simply come here tonight to ask you to allow our group to join the end of the march and commemorate women raped in war.

ALF
Sure, sure. Why not?

MILLIE
You mean it? Really?

ALF
Sure, sure. And let's have a group marching for all the cats who died in the war. And what about birds struck by military aircraft? Think of those poor seagulls.

MILLIE
Now you're being flippant. Surely, you're not comparing comfort women to seagulls.

ROSEMARY
In fact this ANZAC Day we're asking you to all wear a white ribbon. Like this one.

> She walks over and gives each of the men a white ribbon. They take one and stare at it. Alf throws his on the floor in disgust.

ALF
I will not be wearing this rubbish on my lapel. I'll be wearing another ribbon. This one!

> He raps his index finger on the tiny horizontal strip of ribbon on his lapel.

ALF
This is the Military Medal. I won this ribbon storming a foxhole in New Guinea with a pistol and club made from the axel from a Willys Jeep.

> He walks over to Percy. He taps the ribbon on his breast.

ALF
And he'll be wearing this ribbon: The Distinguished Flying Cross. These are the bloody ribbons we'll be wearing on our day Dr Smith. Perhaps I'll take your ribbon home. And I'll burn it with the rest of the trash.

> Rosemary, taken aback, hands a white ribbon to Bev.

ROSEMARY
Will you at least wear one? I didn't catch your name?

ALF
She's just the barmaid. She's not involved in this discussion.

BEV
"She" does have a name... *Hulloooo*. (To Rosemary) Hi, I'm Beverly. People round here call me "Bev", "luv", 'luvvy", "sweetheart", "sugar tits" on account of me magnificent rack - or sometimes click their fingers like I'm a dog. That's when I ignore 'em and slip detergent in their beer.

ROSEMARY
God. Why stay here?

BEV
I steal from the till.

> Kevin laughs out loud.

> Bev winks at Kevin.

KEVIN
You do have a nice rack, Bev, now you mention it. Best tits in the joint.

> Rosemary rolls her eyes in disgust.

ROSEMARY
This is the 1980s. You don't have to put up with a sexist remark like that in the workplace, anymore, Beverly.

BEV
Sure. But I do have a killer rack. Sadly it's heading south but. Will need a wheelbarrow just to walk to the shops, soon. (to Rosemary) So if I wear this white ribbon, I'm supporting women, right?

ROSEMARY
Yes if you wear that ribbon you'll be standing with us.

ALF
(pointing at her)
If you wear that ribbon you'll be fired.

> Bev, opens Rosemary's hand and places the ribbon in her palm.

BEV
You heard the man. God, has spoken. Sorry luv. But I need to make the rent.

> We hear an announcement over the intercom.
>
> *Licence number BZX284 you've left your lights on. It's a lime green Holden Gemini.*
>
> Punter runs across the stage jangling keys.

MILLIE
So you won't support us, Pop?

                                              Alf is speechless. He drinks some beer. Takes a breath. Collects himself.

ALF
(quietly)
Milliscent Parker, you have brought a black cloud into this family by trying to spoil our sacred day. This man (to Percy) piloted over 50 missions in a Lancaster Bomber over the skies of Europe. Not only did he-

ROSEMARY
(emphatically)
Did you bomb Dresden?

PERCY
Pardon?

ROSEMARY
I said "did you bomb Dresden"?

                                                Percy is shocked. He looks at his comrades.

                                                There is a long silence. Percy nervously arranges his cravat.

PERCY
(quietly)
Yes, I bombed Dresden.

MORRIS
Were you in that show, Purce? Dresden?

> Percy is picked up by a spotlight.

PERCY
Yes. Late in the war. February '45. I was with the 722 RAF by then.

I believe 25,000 people died in that single raid. We dropped incendiaries, you see. Created a terrible fire storm. A lot of the buildings in the city centre were wooden structures. So the city burned. And people burned. We had no sense of that. Up there in the stars. Stars that glinted with the promise of freedom. I think a lot about Dresden. My wife and I visited Dresden before the war. The city was known as the 'Jewel Box' because of its baroque and rococo city centre. It was quite unique.

ROSEMARY
Before your lot wiped it off the face of the earth.

ALF
"Your lot!?" Your lot!! Listen, we don't apologise for giving you the freedom you enjoy today. It was *total* war. Some fought it with a bomb from 20,000 feet. Others with a bayonet at 20 feet. In the heat of battle a soldier shows little mercy.

MILLIE
Does that apply to women, too, Pop?

ALF
Bloody women?? We hardly saw any women. The only women we saw in New Guinea were nurses or niggers.

ROSEMARY
(open-mouthed- to Millie)
Did he just say what I thought he said?

PERCY
You said the 'n' word, Alf.

ALF
Nurses?

PERCY
(shaking his head)
Forget it.

KEVIN
Funny. You can say 'fuck' but you can't say 'Gook' or-

ALF
(furious - to Kevin)
Ladies present!

KEVIN
(winks before dropping his shades over his eyes)
I think they call that 'irony', girls.

>Rosemary shakes her head in disbelief.

>Bev points to Millie's bulge.

BEV
Boy or a girl?

MILLIE
We'll find out on the day.

PERCY
A Kinder Surprise.

MORRIS
That's a chocolate egg with a toy in it, right? I bought one for my grandson.

ROSEMARY
Kinder is also the German word for children.

PERCY
Yes.

ROSEMARY
Bet you dropped a few Kinder Surprises on the children of Dresden, that evening.

ALF
See!? This is why you can't march with us! You have no respect for our service. That man had a job to do. He risked his life for you. Night after bloody night!

ROSEMARY
Women died in that war, too, Mr Watson.

ALF
Don't lecture me about women dying in the war. My sister was a nurse in Singapore. The hospital ship was torpedoed by the Japs during the evacuation. The Japanese marched my sister and all the rescued nurses down into the sea and machine gunned the bloody lot of 'em. Japs bayoneted the survivors bobbing in the water. My sister died bravely. She knew what was going to happen as she stood shivering in the sea in her uniform. They all did.

MILLIE
You said Aunt Helen was killed in the war but I didn't know...

ALF
There's a lot you don't know about this war you so despise, Milliscent Parker. There's a lot we never told you. A lot we simply didn't want to talk about. Wanted to forget. Your aunt died for freedom. She died for you and your unborn child. Yes, she died like a lot of people I knew and loved in that God-awful war. Men *and* women.

> Millie needs to sit down. She is feeling faint.

PERCY
Do you need a glass of water, luvvy?

> Bev returns with a glass of water.

MILLIE
You can't imagine they would machine gun nurses...

ALF
That's war, Milliscent. No occupational health and safety. No positive discrimination. But plenty of equal opportunities to *die*. War is simply a long and ugly fight to the death.

ROSEMARY
But like so many events during the war, Dresden was completely unnecessary.

ALF
(blue with rage)

45

Unnecessary? What do you think Hitler would have done if boys like Percy hadn't stopped his war machine? Tell him about the Me262.

KEVIN
What was that? A rifle?

> Percy nods to himself in memory.

PERCY
We were flying over Holland one afternoon on our way to bomb a ball-bearing factory in Stuttgart.

MORRIS
(to the women)
Without bearings nothing moves. War stops.

PERCY
I peak down from the cockpit to see this German fighter taking off at incredible speed. Never seen anything like it. He was on us in a flash and firing both barrels. Took out one of the port engines. But you could fly a Lanc on three engines. Marvellous things. Yes jet engines. The Nazis were a nation of scientists and engineers. Clever race. They'd developed jet technology in the thirties. If they would have had jets in the air during the Battle of Britain, our 'Finest Hour' would have been our 'Final Hour'.

ALF
And what about Hitler's vengeance weapons?

PERCY
Our squadron was stationed at Cricklewood when Hitler first sent them over. Primarily to inflict terror. Doodlebugs we called 'em. You were alright if you heard the noise of the motor. It was

when the engine stopped that your heart was in your throat. Then you'd hear an enormous explosion. People screaming. The V2s were even worse. You never heard them coming. Would take out an entire block. Pilots shot some of them down but if you got too close. Boom!

MILLIE
How terrifying.

ALF
(exacerbated)
We only tell you this Milliscent because you need to understand what that time in our lives was like for us all. How utterly desperate it was. Why we can't forget. Why this march is sacred. It might have been forty years ago but it feels like yesterday.

PERCY
A lot of my friends died trying to save London from those Doodlebugs.

MORRIS
That's when people did their bit. Not like today. In the war we saw brave men. Fine men.

ROSEMARY
Brutal men. This wouldn't have happened if women were running the world. Turn on the news, gentlemen. Women aren't raping. Women aren't killing!

ALF
(raises his walking stick)
Have you heard of a little grocer's daughter called Margaret Thatcher?

MORRIS
(nodding)
The Ironing Lady.

BEV
The *Iron* lady.

ALF
The *Iron* Lady! As is "made of iron". Steely enough to make the tough decisions. Take on the unions. The miners. Lazy people holding Britain back.

BEV
The bloody workers you mean!?

ALF
And what would you know about it?

BEV
(leaning in)
I'm on me break!

MORRIS
I always thought it was the 'Ironing Lady'. I heard she took in ironing at one stage. In the early days.

ALF
Why would the Prime Minister of England take in ironing, fool?

MORRIS
(shrugs)
Cash-in-hand?

                                    Alf shakes his head.

PERCY
(touching his own ear)
You really need to get that contraption looked at, Morrie.

BEV
Ever considered one of them new cochlear implants?

MORRIS
No, I read they're bringing out a new pill called Viagra.

ALF
So Dr Smith, who do you think gave the orders to destroy the General Belgrano?

MORRIS
She killed a general?

ALF
It was a Argentinean battle ship! (sotto voce) Do keep up!

                              Kevin jumps to his feet.

KEVIN
(sings/plays)
Don't cry for me, I've got tinea,
My feet are old and smelly
I ran so far to
Sit beside you.
I'll take my shoes off,
Please keep your distance.

ALF
So help me God... If you don't-

BEV
That's right! Old Madge told 'em to sink it. I remember, now! Good fer her!

ROSEMARY
And she sent 323 men to their death.

ALF
And a bloody good thing it was too. Taking our island in the South Atlantic.

ROSEMARY
You're island?

ALF
The cheek of those dagoes.

ROSEMARY
You're *Australian* not British, Mr Watson.

ALF
I'm a member of the British Empire. The Commonwealth. As you bloody are.

PERCY
I think we all need to take a deep breath.

> A man (PUNTER) dressed in a Salvation Army uniform walks over, thrusting a money box at the boys.

SALVO
Money for the Salvos!

MORRIS
(digging in his pocket)
Any tips for Randwick this Saturday?

SALVO
(leans and winks)
Kings Folly in the 2nd race.

>The money box is passed around.

MORRIS
(putting coins in box)
Good old Salvos. (To Millie) They were there on the front line, you know? Making sandwiches and tea for the men.

ALF
Nearly go themselves shot to pieces in '42 when Toby came back half crazed after a fighting patrol.

PERCY
Why?

ALF
Thought the Japs had taken the camp. Cocked his Owen-gun ready to fire till I stopped him. (Alf points to the Salvo logo and the Japanese flag in the memorabilia cabinet.) The red flag. Very similar from a distance.

>Rosemary places $20 in the box and grabs the man's hand and smiles warmly. They all notice.

MORRIS
(to Rosemary)
Was your family in the war, luv?

ROSEMARY
I'd prefer if you didn't call me "luv" "luvvy" "poppet" or "darling". I prefer Dr Smith or Mz Smith, if you must call me anything.

Morris shrinks.

BEV
(to Kevin)
She wouldn't last long here, would she Kev?

Kevin chuckles, nodding.

MORRIS
Why the "Mzzz?" If you don't mind me asking.

PERCY
Yes, why is that?

ROSEMARY
Why should I have to define my marital status each time I introduce myself?

BEV
I agree, sister. And if you met me ex-husband, you'd understand.

MORRIS
Fair point. Well made.

ALF
(to Rosemary)
Wearing blue stockings today, are we?

BEV
(coquettishly hitching her skirt)
Kinky devil. I'm wearing me Razzamatazz.

ALF
(sneering)
She knows what I mean.

ROSEMARY
(to Alf)
I should do. I teach modern history. (To Bev) The Blue Stockings Society was a women's social and educational movement in England in the mid-18th century. It was established to promote the education of women.

MORRIS
So were they? Your family? In the war, I mean?

ROSEMARY
Yes. My parents came out from England in the mid '50s.

PERCY
Ten Pound Poms.

ROSEMARY
Not exactly. Yes, dad was British. He was at Dunkirk. He later served with the commandos. Ran patrols across the channel or something-

ALF
Or *something*?

ROSEMARY
(dryly)
Yes, it was risky business, I suppose. I'll grant you that.

ALF
I'm sure it was Mzzz Smith.

PUNTER
Can you mind me machine while I have a piss?

ALF
Ladies present!

PUNTER
It's gonna pay a jackpot. I can feel it in me waters. But I need a leak.

ALF
I've told you before. Get lost! We're in a board meeting. Strike me pink!

> The punter 'ums and ahhs', hops from one leg to the other before returning to the machine crossing his legs.

MORRIS
(to Rosemary)
Go on.

ROSEMARY
Anyway, Mum said Dad had his boat shot out from under him a few times. Funny enough, Mum knew long before being officially told because she bought a Ouija board and a spirit told her "he was in the water" so she says.

KEVIN
Spooky.

MORRIS
The occult was very big in the war.

PERCY
A lot of sudden deaths do that to people.

ROSEMARY
Anyway, after the war, he was offered free passage to Australia with his family for his war service.

ALF
And quite right too. That's the stock we want to build our nation. Not these bloody dagoes and what not. And now this Cambodian refugee trash.

PERCY
Go on, dear.

ROSEMARY
Well, he was an alcoholic. Mum migrated to Australia hoping he'd change. A new start. But coming to Australia to stop drinking was like sending Dracula to the blood bank. Dad became a hopeless drunk.

KEVIN
(nodding to others)
Repression.

ROSEMARY
No doubt.

KEVIN
He needed music.

ROSEMARY
He needed courage.

ALF
What!?

ROSEMARY
Not in war. But in life. You see, he abandoned our family almost upon arrival. Left them on the migrant hostel in Cabramatta where we all lived in a tin Nissen hut for nearly ten years. Mum brought us up - four children on her own on that stinking dusty hostel. She was *my* hero. But there's no grand parade for her. No medal.

PERCY
I've seen it happen. Good men turn to drink.

MORRIS
Some turn to the horses.

BEV
Some turn to the ukulele.

>   Kevin strums a chord.

ALF
(menacingly to Kevin)
Some turn to extreme violence.

>   With a grimace, Kevin puts the ukulele under the table.

ROSEMARY
He never drank before the war, Mum said. But seeing your best mate's head blown off at Dunkirk would change things, I imagine.

Was never the same after the war, Mum said.

KEVIN
Been there. Done that. Got the T-Shirt.

ROSEMARY
You were at Dunkirk?

KEVIN
Do I look like I piss into a bag? I'm only 40!

MORRIS
(outraged)
That was said in confidence!

> We faintly hear the soundtrack of a Yuletide melody played on a toy piano.
>
> Kevin removes his Ray-Bans.

KEVIN
I was on the turps in a little tittie bar in Saigon called *Nips*. Actually, that's where I met Curly Shirley.

ALF
Ladies present!

BEV
(winks)
Tell me later, Handsome.

KEVIN
Anyway, my story also takes place at Christmas. But the Gooks never celebrated Christmas. They were all Buddhists. But it was

a special time for us, of course. A time when we'd miss our families, an that. So being Chrissie, we were all on the drink, carrying on like drunken Aussies - as you do when you're abroad. Laughing. Swearing. Carrying on like gooses. Tonk was lighting his farts at the bar. Gaz was dropping his schlong in Freddo's beer. As you do abroad, you know...

ROSEMARY
(dryly)
As you do.

KEVIN
Anyway, suddenly, a little Gook kid brings us a Chrissie present. It's all wrapped in glittery paper, an that. We open the card. The card reads *Merry Christmas D Company*. The card is one of those tacky cards that plays a little sour Christmas tune when you open it. Anyway, Gaz lights a cigar - he loved cigars - and walks outside to open the gift. Says over his shoulder, "I bet it's that crap coffee they all drink". BOOM! Takes his head clean off. If he hadn't walked outside with it, I wouldn't be telling you this story.

>   Kevin puts his Ray-Bans back
>   on and picks up his ukulele.

MILLIE
That's a terrible story. I'm sorry.

KEVIN
Yeah. Poor old, Gaz. Never *did* have a head for drink.

>   Kevin improvises a song.

KEVIN
(singing/playing)

Ping Pong Suzie.
Was a little floozy.
Never had a...
Um...never had a...
never had a....

> Kevin gets up and throws the ukulele across the room.
>
> Lights out.

ACT 1 SCENE 2

> The RSL Club. Some months later.
>
> Lights are raised. Alf, Kevin and Morris are perched at their usual table in the club. The older men are in their usual sombre suits.
>
> We see a sign draped across the bar reading: *Happy Easter*. The stage is festooned with Easter decorations.
>
> Morris tweaks his hearing aid.
>
> Alf is holding a gladstone bag.

ALF
Look at this! It's all in the bloody newspapers. Strike me pink!

MORRIS
What is?

ALF
This 'women raped in war' business. It's all they can talk about. Bloody disgrace.

MORRIS
Absentees: Cess Roberts, he's got gout due to-

ALF
Not now, Morris. We need to sort this protest business out before next week's march. Milliscent has asked to see us for a final meeting.

KEVIN
Are you two speaking to each other these days?

ALF
No. But she's coming in tonight in a final effort to convince us. However, I've decided to give it to her warts and all. Something I've never done before.

> Alf places the bag on the table.

MORRIS
What do you mean?

> We hear an announcement over the intercom.
>
> *Will Harold please collect his dentures from reception?*

> Bev - wearing rabbit ears hat - brings over drinks and a plate of sushi.

ALF
Why aren't we in the bloody boardroom this time?

BEV
Being painted.

ALF
Strike me pink!

> She lays some soy sauce and wasabi on the table.

BEV
"Wall St Grey", actually.

> Punter whizzes past holding aloft a pair of dentures

ALF
(pointing at sushi)
What's this rubbish?

BEV
Sushi.

ALF
What?

BEV
It's Japanese. Very trendy at the moment.

ALF
For the love of Mike! What did we fight this bloody war for? If we are not driving their rubbish cars we're eating their stinking food?

BEV
If yous don't want it I'll keep it for me tea.

>Percy enters, but does a double-take at the cabinet.

PERCY
(flagging them over)
Have you seen this? Come and have a look.

>Alf, Morris and Kevin follow Percy to the sacred shrine that is the display cabinet that holds the war memorabilia. Alf throws his walking stick to the floor.

ALF
THIS IS THE LAST BLOODY STRAW!

>The quartet return to their table.

BEV
So did you want the complementary sushi?

>Alf takes the plate of sushi and hurls it across the room.
>
>At this moment Millie enters the stage - all 'billy business' and ready for action. However, when

> she sees her grandfather's outburst, she is shocked.
>
> In her lapel she wears the white ribbon.
> Millie is now heavily pregnant.

BEV
(to Alf, dryly)
So was that takeaway or eat here?

> Bev silently cleans it up.

MILLIE
(nervously)
Everything alright, Pop? You seem upset.

> Rosemary enters the stage, breathless.

ROSEMARY
Sorry I'm late Mill. Have you heard the news?

MILLIE
No? What news?

ALF
Where *is* it?

MILLIE
Where's *what?*

ALF
I want it back. NOW!

ROSEMARY
(sotto voce to Millie)
What's he on about?

> Alf lcads Mille and Rosemary to the display cabinet of war artefacts.

MILLIE
What's wrong?

> Alf leans into the cabinet and removes an artefact. He holds it up to the light.

ALF
Someone has broken into this cabinet and switched my bayonet for this!

PERCY
What is it?

BEV
Looks like a curling wand.

> Rosemary smothers a laugh. Millie is open-mouthed.

MILLIE
Pop, I give you my word I know nothing about it.

> They return to the table.
>
> Bev joins them and has a drink.

ALF
Well what about *this?*

Alf throws a newspaper on the table at Millie.

MILLIE
What is it, Pop?

ALF
All the newspapers can write about is this bloody ridiculous protest of yours next week. It's *our* day. Our day of remembrance. A solemn day.

ROSEMARY
A solemn day for *all* victims of war.

ALF
Oh it's Miss Bluestocking again. Do you have to drag her along every time?

BEV
Dr Bluestocking.

ALF
(to Rosemary)
Stealing is a criminal offence.

MILLIE
Pop someone's playing a practical joke. I really need you understand that we are not dishonouring your service. Nothing could be further from the truth. We're proud of what you achieved. We simply want to join the march with your blessing to commemorate these forgotten women.

> Bev smiles and winks a 'good for you' at her.

ROSEMARY
You're wasting your breath, Mil. (to Alf) Tell her Mr President...

MILLIE
(to Alf)
Tell me what?

ROSEMARY
Ever heard of Section 23A of the Traffic Ordinance?

MILLIE
No.

ROSEMARY
You wouldn't have because it was being rushed through last night. Forget asking for them to change their mind whether we can join the march. This new law means if any of us march on the day, we'll be instantly arrested. Let me read it to you.

> Rosemary produces a sheet of paper.

ROSEMARY
(reading)
After section (23) of the Traffic Ordinance 1937, the following section is inserted:
23a - where a person is taking part, or attempts to take part, in an ANZAC Day Parade, and there are reasonable grounds for believing that the person is likely to commit an offence against sub-section (3), a member of the Australian Federal Police of or above the rank of Sergeant may direct the person not to take part

in the parade. A person who contravenes a direction given under sub-section (1) is guilty of an offence.

MILLIE
Pop, you've changed the *laws* to stop us remembering these women? Has it come to this?

> Alf grins like the cat that swallowed the canary.

BEV
(slowly nodding)
Sly old fox.

KEVIN
(taps his nose at Bev)
Pays to know people in low places.

MILLIE
Pop, how could you? All this time you've been stalling us.

ROSEMARY
Welcome to the Boys Club, Mil. That's how it works.

MILLIE
You mean they're going to arrest 200 women? They're going to arrest *me*?

PERCY
Well, obviously you won't be marching, luvvy. Not in your condition.

MILLIE
I wasn't going to march but I sure as hell am now. Try and stop me!

ROSEMARY
That's the spirit Mil!

ALF
(To Rosemary)
You stay out of this. Are you going to let this man-hater influence all your decisions? What about the health of my first great-grandchild?

MILLIE
Is that all you're worried about, Pop? Your grandchild? Why not start worrying about the people who bring them into the world. *Women.* The *same* women who are raped, bashed, murdered, abused in this city every single day. The victims of domestic violence. The victims of unspeakable crimes.

ALF
Now you're being melodramatic.

MILLIE
Am I, Pop? Did you know every week a woman is murdered by her current or former male partner? Women walk around this city in fear of their lives, Pop.

ROSEMARY
In fact, why not simply turn to page 8 of today's paper, Mr Watson?

>Alf picks up the newspaper and turns to a page.

ALF
(reading)
Alan Bond talks about new mystery keel. I don't give a tinker's cuss about yachts.

ROSEMARY
Beneath that. The small story.

ALF
(reading)
Local schoolgirl missing.

ROSEMARY
Raped and murdered.

MORRIS
How do you know that?

ROSEMARY
Statistics.

BEV
She's right.

PERCY
They found blood on her schoolbag, the news said last night. Looks grim. Poor pet.

ALF
Listen, I agree with you. It's bloody *shameful* how some men treat women at times.

MILLIE
Don't you see Pop? Your war was over 40 years ago. Ours is never-ending.

ALF
So what is this all about then? Is it about women in the war? Or women today?

ROSEMARY
It's the same thing. Remembering these women is one way of affecting change, Mr Watson. It's about ending *our* war.

ALF
You're preaching to the converted, Mzzzzz Smith.

ROSEMARY
Do you have to do that every time?

ALF
Do what?

ROSEMARY
"Mzzz Smith"?

BEV
Dentures.

MILLIE
It's demeaning, Pop.

> Alf slams his walking stick on the table.

ALF
Demeaning? *Demeaning*!? I'll tell you what's demeaning. Disrupting our march and dishonouring people who fought for your bloody freedom. (sotto voce) Strike me pink! (to Millie) Can't you have your *own* march? On your own day? On International Women's Day or something?

KEVIN
Man bites dog.

PERCY
What?

BEV
March on International Women's Day no one notices. March on ANZAC day everyone notices.

KEVIN
Man bites dog.

ALF
What *are* you babbling on about?

KEVIN
Dog bites man: no story. Man bites dog: a story.

MORRIS
I had a dog in Tobruk. Was left behind by the Italians when we drove them out in the first attack. A little tag made from a cartridge on his neck said 'Cucciolo'.

ROSEMARY
Puppy.

MORRIS
What?

PERCY
He's deaf, luv. Sorry Mz Smith. (loud voice to Morris) She says "was it a puppy?"

ROSEMARY
No. Cucciolo. It means puppy in Italian.

MORRIS
She's right. Do you speak Italian, luv?

ROSEMARY
Please don't call me "luv".

MORRIS
Sorry Mz Smith.

MILLIE
Rosemary speaks seven languages.

BEV
So do I.

MILLIE
Really?

BEV
(nodding)
After a bottle of vodka I can speak up to thirteen.

ALF
You're a clever girl, Mzzz Smith.

ROSEMARY
I'm not a girl. I'm a woman, Mr Watson.

MILLIE
(softly, to Rosemary)
Rosie, this is not helping.

ROSEMARY
What's the point now?

ALF
We could have used you in the war. Translator. You see, a lot of women died fighting this filthy men's war you so despise. Ever heard of a little nurse called Nancy Wake? The Gestapo called her The White Mouse. Let's call 'Old Nance' and see what she has to say about all this. Her husband was murdered by the Gestapo. Nancy killed plenty of Germans in "our filthy men's war".

MILLIE
Like I said to you in my letter, Pop, it's not about dishonouring your service. I'm proud of what you did. It's about affecting change. Making people-

ALF
It should be about young people acknowledging our service. Our sacrifice. Teaching them some bloody core ethics. Even the granddaughters of those who served.

ROSEMARY
How does a bunch of 20-somethings getting completely pie-eyed on shots on ANZAC Day commemorate your comrades, Mr Watson? Do tell me.

> Percy smiles and nods quietly to himself.

BEV
(lighting a cigarette)
She's got a point, Alf. The rivers of vomit in the toilets are something the Dam Busters would be proud of.

MILLIE
Why *should* some young person get completely smashed on ANZAC Day, Pop? What does that say about our culture? What

73

does it say about your service? If anything, it disrespects your service, if it's the solemn day you say it is.

BEV
It's not *all* mindless drinking.

MILLIE
Really?

BEV
There's a commemorative element. Occasionally, they'll glass someone on the way home.

KEVIN
True.

ALF
Haven't you got work to do, Miss Vander-whats-it...?

BEV
I'm on me break.

> She pours herself a drink.

PERCY
She's right, you know, Alf.

ALF
What?

PERCY
In fact, that's why Cess doesn't march anymore, he told me, just quietly.

MORRIS
And these children marching with their grandfather's medals. Bit silly.

ALF
(shocked)
Have you all lost your senses? It's *wonderful*! The fact that they are remembering their Pop's service. (to Millie) Unlike some young people who couldn't give a tinker's cuss about their forefathers-

PERCY
(quietly)
It was very moving once. In the twenties, I mean. All those poor mothers weeping into their lace hankies along the high street. I can still see them. Mum was one of them.

ALF
Your father was a surgeon at Gallipoli, wasn't he, Purce?

PERCY
(nodding)
Shot in the neck at Pine Ridge. They say he was desperately trying to bandage himself right up until the end. Found him pooled in his own blood with all his field medical kit out around him.

BEV
I'm sorry to hear that, Percy.

PERCY
If I'm honest, I've got mixed feelings about all these young people going to Gallipoli each year. Getting completely drunk and fornicating on the graves of our fathers in order to celebrate 'Australia's victory over the Nazis'.

MORRIS
They fought the Turks.

ROSEMARY
(smiling)
That's the subtext.

KEVIN
(to Bev)
You know I walked into the pantry yesterday and found the ANZAC biscuits fighting with the Turkish Delights.

ALF
Will you belt up?

KEVIN
(to Alf)
Had to send in the Scotch Fingers to restore order.

MILLIE
Was your father in the war, Kevin?

KEVIN
Yes.

PERCY
Where was he in the conflict?

KEVIN
Casino.

PERCY
He fought the Germans in Italy?

KEVIN
(deadpan)
No, he was a chronic gambler.

> We hear an announcement.
>
> *Tonight badge draw is member number 2018. That's number 2018. You have ten minutes to collect your prize which has jackpotted to $530.*

PERCY
At any rate, my father worked a lot with Aboriginal communities in the bush. I feel that, rather than see all these young people sending all their money to the Turkish government each year, I know Dad would rather see these same young people go to a remote Aboriginal community and teach kids to read for a week.

ALF
(blue with rage)
You're talking like a bloody communist!

PERCY
I'm simply expressing an opinion, Alf. It's still a democracy, I believe.

MORRIS
That can happen if you watch too much ABC. (to Alf) I only ever watch the test cricket.

ALF
Well, I never thought I'd hear the day when one of our war heroes, a man who won the DFC-

PERCY
Alf, we don't have a monopoly on the word: hero. Heroes are *also* people who raise foster children. Heroes are people who fight for refugees. Heroes are people who go to outback communities and - like I said - teach Aboriginal children to read and write so they have a future in this sunny bloody democracy of ours. Gallipoli is about looking at the past. It's time we looked to the future. We have a lot of work ahead of us.

ALF
(to Morris)
Strike me pink! He's turned into bloody Castro.

> Rosemary walks over to Percy and kisses him on the forehead before sitting down.

PERCY
(chuckling, shyly)
Well, I haven't been kissed by a young woman for a while.

MILLIE
You see, Rosie. Don't give up just yet!

ALF
(to Percy, disgusted)
And you call yourself a member of the RSL.

PERCY
(jumping to his feet)
I call myself a member of the RSL because I flew 65 missions over Europe. I'm entitled to my view. Does Morris have to hand in his badge because he votes for the Democrats?

MORRIS
(also jumps to his feet)
That was said in confidence!

PERCY
So don't tell me how to think. I was dodging night fighters and weaving through flak over the skies of Europe while you were sunning yourself on some bloody tropical island.

> Alf slams his walking- stick on the table.

ALF
Tropical *island*!!

> Bev sneaks a shot of gin from a hanging bottle and sculls it.

BEV
(to Millie)
Oh-oh. Ladies you may wish to sample some of my cordial. It's gonna get ugly.

> Millie shakes her head and points to her belly.
>
> Rosemary shakes her head also.

ALF
Tropical island!? *Tropical bloody island?* Of all the nerve!

MORRIS
Purce, I think you should apologise-

ALF
I wasn't fighting the enemy from 20,000 feet, sitting on a silk parachute!

PERCY
How *dare* you!

MORRIS
Now listen, Alf. This is getting silly. You were both heroes.

KEVIN
(to the women)
The Dalai Lama says "The true hero is one who conquers his own anger and hatred."

PERCY
Well, certainly I didn't wait till '41 to join the reserve hoping to unload trucks in Darwin. I joined in '39. Like every decent red-blooded Australian. (sotto voce) Bloody Chocko.

ALF
(to Millie)
See what you've done. You're turning us against each other now. Happy!?

KEVIN
(to Bev)
It's all in the breathing. I learned a lot about Buddhism in Nam. Kevin takes a yoga-style breath.

ALF
Unlike you, Percy, I was fighting the enemy hand to hand. Bayonet to bayonet!

BEV
(to the women)
You should see him at the carvery.

ALF
Be quiet, will you? I'm trying to make a point.

> Bev salutes and takes a slug of her gin. She passes a shot to Kevin.

KEVIN
(to Bev)
The Dalai Lama doesn't drink. That's where we part ways. (drinks) A spiritual impasse.

> Kevin pauses before taking a slug and pulls a face.

MILLIE
You were fighting at Kokoda, weren't you, Pop?

ALF
That's right. Fighting for my bloody life. Fighting for 46 men's lives, in fact.

BEV
(to Alf)
So what did you do before the war, Alf?

ALF
(menacingly)
Work for a living. Something quite foreign to you.

BEV
I'm on me break!

PERCY
(winking)
My taxes.

ALF
(chuckling)
Yes, I did his taxes. That's where we met, Percy?

PERCY
(wry smile)
That's right.

ALF
Our firm did your uncle's books. Before you left for Europe. Your uncle was a GP. Had a practice here in Gosford, if I recall.

ROSEMARY
So was that your profession, too, Mr Scott? GP?

PERCY
No. After the war I became a pilot for Ansett.

MORRIS
'Lot easier than flying a Lancaster bomber, I imagine.

PERCY
(chuckles)
Quite right. Had some rough weather over Adelaide once in '64. The passengers were jumpy. A woman started screaming hysterically. Children were crying. I calmly announced over the intercom that I've flown in much worse weather than this and

with a Messerschmitt 109 up my backside. The crew all laughed. Passengers laughed. Relieved the tension.

ROSEMARY
What was your profession, Mr Watson? Bookkeeper?

ALF
Accountant. I was working in a large accounting firm in the city when I joined the militia. We all felt it was only a matter of time till the Japs attacked the mainland. They desperately needed supplies, you see. Before the Battle of the Coral Sea - where we defeated the Japanese naval invasion of Moresby - things looked grim for us. We all decided that if they attacked the mainland in force, we'd fight them to the death. But the reserve all thought we were safe from being sent overseas to fight for some miserable piece of desert in Africa.

MORRIS
Hey!

ALF
No offence, Morris.

>   Morris relaxes.

ALF
You see, by that stage of the war, we were more concerned with Tojo in our backyard.

MORRIS
Yes, they couldn't send the militia to Europe. It was against the law.

MILLIE
But they sent you to New Guinea.

ALF
A loophole.

BEV
Loophole?

MILLIE
I don't understand.

ROSEMARY
New Guinea was an Australian protectorate in the 1940s.

MORRIS
Our own little colony in the Pacific.

ALF
New Guinea was originally part of the German Colonial Empire until we took it in 1914. The 'Imperial German Pacific Protectorates' included the German Solomon Islands - Buka, Bougainville, the Carolines, Palau, the Marianas, the Marshall Islands and the remote island of Nauru.

BEV
Nauru?

KEVIN
Never heard of it.

ALF
Probably never will. Total land mass of the German Pacific Empire at the time - now let me do the math - was... 249,500 square kilometres.

MORRIS
(winking to Millie)

Always was good with numbers, your Pop.

PERCY
That's why we made him president of the club.

BEV
(dryly)
You should see him at Keno.

MORRIS
Club's been in the black for over 20 years. Was haemorrhaging money until Chocko Watson took over.

MILLIE
Chocko?

> We hear an announcement.
>
> *Stick around for the swinging sounds of Ronnie Stevens and Crush. They'll entertain you with hits from the 60s and 70s. So sit back, relax and put on your dancing shoes and get ready to boogie.*
>
> Alf looks up and shakes his head.

ALF
Yes. They called us "Chokos".

MILLIE
Earlier Percy called you that. In the pejorative. What does it mean, Pop?

ALF
Chocolate soldiers. We were supposed to melt like chocolate at the sight of the enemy.

MORRIS
(smiling)
But you didn't.

ALF
We didn't. (smiles with memory) And you know we didn't, Morris because you were there.

ROSEMARY
(to Morris)
I don't understand. You said you were in Tobruk.

MORRIS
I was. But after we defeated the Italians at El Alamein, Curtain demanded our troops back to fight the more immediate threat breathing down our neck at home.

PERCY
Churchill refused.

MORRIS
Churchill never liked Australians. Thought we were "poor stock".

PERCY
The convict stain, and all that. Said Britain would take back Australia from the Japanese after the war. When they got around to it.

ALF
Yes. (sighs) We all felt let down by the great man. After everything we did for the mother country in the first big shout.

Can you possibly imagine what they would have done to us? The Japs? To people like your Nanna, Millie? They'd executed your Aunt in Singapore. Beheaded the neighbour's boy at Changi-

ROSEMARY
We know now that the Japanese never intended to take Australia, Mr Watson.

ALF
Hindsight is a wonderful thing, Mzzz Smith. But this was 1942. They'd smashed Singapore. Bombed Darwin. Torpedoed Sydney Harbour. (to Millie) Even shelled your cousin's flat at Bondi. People were scared out of their wits. So the 7th Army was sent back to Australia to stop the Japanese reaching Moresby. But they were taking too bloody long to get there. The Japs would have taken Moresby by the time the 7th reached the port. Would have wiped them out as they landed.

MORRIS
So their job was to stop the Japanese from reaching Moresby until we - the 7th - arrived.

ALF
I had a degree in accounting. Had several employees at the accounting firm. So they made me an officer, would you believe? Never even held a rifle before. Bloody joke.

PERCY
Really? I didn't know that.

ALF
Yes. And here I was telling drovers and bushmen-

PERCY
Why didn't you join up in '39? I've always resented you over that, if I'm honest.

ALF
Wouldn't take me.

MORRIS
Reserved occupation.

ALF
(nods)
Reserved occupation. We were doing the navy's books, would you believe?

PERCY
Why not quit?

ALF
If I walked out, many men - older men who'd been with the firm for years with families - would have lost their jobs. We were still reeling from the Depression. But after my sister was murdered, I joined the militia. What you'd call the reserve now. And off we went to stop the Japanese: an accountant, a botanist with a PhD in tropical orchids, and a concert pianist who they'd made lieutenant because he had a bachelor degree from the Royal Academy of Music.

MORRIS
Who was that?

ALF
Old Toby.

PERCY
Have you heard him play Rachmaninoff? His hands are a blur.

A spotlight picks up Alf.

ALF
Nearly had them shot off when he went to light three cigarettes off one match one evening. As he went to light the third, I knocked the match out of his hand. Bullet grazed his knuckle. Wally was shot dead through the eye. You see, we were constantly being picked off by snipers on the track. So enough was enough. The following morning, I set to work. From the trajectory of the bullet I did some calculations. Our friend's bullet lodged into a palm tree beside our tent. So after some basic trigonometry, I calculated that our friend must be hiding in the fifth palm tree on a ridge above Templeton's Crossing. I took a platoon with me to have a quiet word with him.

MILLIE
A quiet word?

ALF
(to Morris and Percy)
He wasn't expecting toast with his breakfast that morning but a flame thrower soon fixed that. He fell from the tree screaming, spinning like a Catherine wheel. Toby took my revolver and shot him dead.

ROSEMARY
How awful.

ALF
Yes it was. We were cranky with him for that. We wanted to see him burn. He'd killed five of our boys that week. But [sighs] if you'd heard Toby play Chopin, you'd understand.

From the old gladstone bag on the table Alf removes an old photograph album. He passes it to Millie.

ALF
You weren't allowed to take photos in the army. But I was always a bit of an amateur photographer before the war. Had my Box Brownie with me on the track. You see, at the top of that page there's a picture of his charred corpse. Funny how the teeth look almost comic.

KEVIN
(singing with ukulele)
Now laughing friends deride
Tears I cannot hide
Oh, so I smile and say
When a lovely flame dies
Smoke gets in your eyes

Alf glares at him.

ALF
Do you think this is funny? Do you think I want to tell my granddaughter all this?

ROSEMARY
(to Kevin)
I notice you always sing or make jokes when you're stressed.

KEVIN
(thinking)
You know...my shrink said that, too.

ALF
So an accountant, a botanist and a concert pianist and 1000 inexperienced men met 10,000 crack Japanese Marines in the jungle. Marines who'd wiped out every army they'd met.

KEVIN
You were outnumbered 10 to one??

ALF
Correct.

KEVIN
That's a tough day at the office.

ALF
We did alright.

MORRIS
(smiling and winking)
You did alright.

ALF
(to Percy)
Yes, we did alright for a battalion of chocolates (turns to others) led by three young men out of their depth and terrified out of their wits. We had quite a few drovers, farmers and bushmen in the militia. Men who taught us bushcraft. They were naturals in the jungle. Quite surprised the Japanese with their fighting. But we had to. Like I said, this enemy offered no quarter. When the Russians surrounded the Germans in a pincer movement over 100,000 men surrendered. But a Jap will fight to the death. There's no surrender.

MORRIS
They were mean, the Japs. Meaner than the Germans. We quite liked the Germans. They took you prisoner. Gave you coffee and a sandwich with the most fantastic mustard. Now, what they could do with cabbage-

MILLIE
I thought Germans were cruel in the war?

MORRIS
Nazis were cruel. Not all Germans were Nazis. Not in the desert, anyway. They say the African Campaign was a war without hate.

ALF
Go on Morris. Tell 'em like it is. That's what today is all about. This is our last chance to knock some sense into these girls before next week's march. I've discussed it with Peggy last night. So please...go ahead. Give it to her warts and all.

> Alf waves him on ceremoniously.

MORRIS
Well, Cucciolo was never really frightened of the bombing. I bloody was. We all were. You weren't human, if you weren't scared. At any rate, one day a bomb landed close. Too close. Hearing's never been the same since. Anyway, piece of shrapnel hit his leg. Poor little thing took off like a rabbit. So that night I went looking for him in No Man's Land. I was picked up by a German patrol. I was then herded in the back of a truck with a group of Australian commandos - what these days you'd call Special Forces.

BEV
So what happened? I've never heard this story before.

MORRIS
Well, they'd blown up a petrol dump that night and had been captured. As you can imagine, they were surprised to see the old mess cook in the truck. They all loved me, you see. In the army, if you couldn't drive a truck or fire a gun they made you a cook. So imagine having a professional chef as the mess cook? They never had it so good. At any rate, these Special Forces fellows were as tough as teak. Before the war I was Head Chef at the Hotel Canberra. When we got back to the prison camp the Germans interrogated us. Wanted to know what British unit we were with. They kept insisting we were British but wearing Australian uniforms, in order to frighten them. They weren't frighted of the British. But they were very concerned about us.

MILLIE
Why? I don't understand.

MORRIS
After we defeated the Italians the Australians became somewhat of a thorn in Rommel's side at Tobruk. But more importantly, it allowed Monty to build up his forces in Alex for the big push. So like your Pop's boys who were the first troops to stop the Japanese advance, we too were the first troops to stop the German advance. Australians. At Tobruk. We didn't fight like the British. In neat rows of gentlemanly columns after gin and tonics at tiffin. We fought mostly at night. Fought like desperate scrambling rats.

ROSEMARY
The Rats of Tobruk.

MORRIS
That's right. When Lord Haw Haw called us that over the radio, we all started drawing rats on our uniforms. On our helmets. Aussie sense of humour, you see. At any rate, it rattled the

Germans. The Poms were there, too. But only the artillery boys. British 3rd Armoured Brigade. All the dirty night time business was carried out by our boys. The grisly hand to hand stuff.

> We hear an announcement over the intercom. Morris pauses.

> *The fishing club is about to start their raffle. The boys in blue have some lovely king prawns to give away so support your local fishing club and buy a raffle ticket.*

MILLIE
I forgot the Italians were in the war. What were the Italians like as soldiers?

MORRIS
Utterly useless. The Eye-tie Army was completely unable to put up an effective resistance. The Italian commander, General Manella, was taken prisoner after only 12 hours of battle, and 24 hours later our boys cleaned up the remaining troops. We only lost 49 dead and 306 wounded. But we captured, would you believe, 27,000 Italian POWs, 208 guns and 28 tanks.

BEV
What a victory! This calls for sambuca!

> Bev leaves them for the bar.

> Bev returns and arranges shots around the table. They all scull them. All except Alf and Millie.

BEV
Compliments of Brian. Go on Morrie. You've never talked about his before.

MORRIS
You see the Italians were all conscripts. They didn't want to be there. They hated Mussolini. They were a nice bunch, really. Happiest playing soccer and drinking wine and cooking. I liked them. Related to them. At any rate, not only did they leave all their supples behind, but their old family recipes! I still have them in a book somewhere. That doesn't mean much today with people like Peter Russell-Clarke and Keith Floyd on TV every five minutes. But in 1940s Australia, we didn't know much about continental cooking.

BEV
When I was a kid spaghetti came in a can.

MORRIS
And you bought Olive Oil at the chemist!

MILLIE
You're kidding?

MORRIS
True.

ALF
Let's not start banging on about food again, Morris.

MORRIS
At any rate, we liked the Germans. But we hated the Japs. If the Germans were like us, the Japs were nothing like us. They were cruel.

ALF
Like Uncle Morrie said, the Japs had never been defeated before in battle. They had God on their side. Not simply ideology and spurious notions of racial purity. We were facing a fanatical people. A people who organised banzai charges at machine guns. A people who held ridges to the death. The Stanley's were impossible.

BEV
Who were they? Brothers?

ALF
It's a mountain range cutting through the jungles of New Guinea. At times we had to fire up at the Japs vertically. Snowy Peters - a shoe salesman at Mark Foys in Sydney - was shot in the top of his foot.

BEV
Not a great career move.

KEVIN
(sings/plays)
There's no business like Shoe Business, there's no business for Snow...

MORRIS
Kev, that's a bit much, mate.

ROSEMARY
Are you finding this stressful, Kevin?

ALF
Our job was to keep them fighting until the AIF arrived. What a desperate task it was. The Japs rained down grenades on us. Mortars. Even poured buckets of excrement on us. And if they

captured you it wasn't bloody coffee and sandwiches with mustard. But the worst was to come.

MILLIE
What could possibly be worse?

ALF
In October '42, two of our forward scouts were killed on a fighting patrol. They'd both been shot by Japs with a machine gun hidden in a fox hole.

> Alf is visibly stressed. He suddenly downs a shot of sambuca.
>
> They all gasp.

ROSEMARY
Go on.

ALF
So they shot these two boys from A company in the 3rd battalion. Fair enough. But when the 2nd 25th patrol came through two days later, they discovered the bodies.

MILLIE
What do mean?

> Alf finds it difficult to talk. Clears his throat.

ALF
Eaten.

MILLIE
Eaten?

ALF
Cannibalised. The fleshy parts of the calves and thighs had been hacked off by a sharp instrument. One scout had both arms removed and other fleshy portions of his body removed.

MILLIE
Dear God.

ALF
The same patrol of the 2nd 25th found a parcel of meat wrapped in a large leaf. The medical officer of the 2/25 confirmed it was human flesh.

KEVIN
I need to get some air.

>   Kevin exits the stage.

>   Millie seems ill.

BEV
I'll fetch you a glass of water, petal.

MILLIE
Thank you.

ALF
Grotesque, isn't it? We came across the bodies in a clearing. The Japs were starving, you see. We'd cut their supply lines.

PERCY
It's what defeated Napoleon.

ALF
They'd overreached. That was our plan. To stretch their supply lines and fight them in depth. New Guinea was one conquest too far for Tojo. So when they ran out of food, they damn well ate us, the bastards. And that's why Mzzz Smith they would have eaten the dog.

> Bev returns with water.

MILLIE
(holding her head)
Do you have any Aspirin, Bev?

> Bev rushes off-stage.
> Alf looks concerned

ALF
(exacerbated)
You wouldn't have to hear about this Milliscent if you didn't insist on this stupid march.

MORRIS
When we arrived we couldn't believe these 'Chockos' fought the enemy all the way in that impossible terrain. When we relieved them, they refused to go. At any rate, when the 7th's commander was told that the Chockos aren't leaving till the Japs are out of New Guinea, he was moved to tears. I know. I was there making his bloody breakfast.

> Bev returns with Aspirin for Millie. She takes it.

ALF
The hardest fighting was around Buna and Gona where the Japs had dug in and were determined to fight to the death to maintain

a foothold in Papua. Terrible fighting. Terrible. A lot of boys never came back. Buried a lot of them along the track so the Japs couldn't eat them.

PERCY
Alf I'd like to apologise for my "sunbaking on a tropical island remark". Someone said you guarded a toilet in the Pacific in the final months of the war.

>Alf roars with laughter.

ALF
No it's true! I was slashed across the thigh by a cross-eyed Japanese Colonel in Buna. Lucky for me he was as blind as a bat without his tiny glasses, which had been knocked off in a banzai charge. I was firing off the hip when my Owen Gun jammed. He was running at me with his samurai sword as mad as a wheel. Didn't have time to reach for my pistol. So he hacked at me like I was sugar cane.

MILLIE
Pop, how terrifying!

ALF
Was rather.

>Alf pours some water, shaken and dry of mouth.

ALF
Anyway, I refused to go home and leave my men so they sent me to the island to guard a latrine to recuperate for a month. You can still see the scar where he slashed me with his sword. In the pelvis. Went right through to the bone.

                    Alf shows Millie the scar.

MILLIE
Nan said you got that mowing the hill when the mower tipped over.

ALF
What would she say to a seven-year-old?

MILLIE
So that samurai sword above the mantelpiece?

ALF
(chuckles)
Never took souvenirs. But I felt I had sharpened it for him.

MILLIE
Good God!

ROSEMARY
What happened to this Japanese soldier who attacked you?

ALF
I managed to knock him off his feet. But pretty soon he was on top of me strangling me. So I pulled out my bayonet and plunged it into his throat. Twisted it until his eyes popped out.

                    Millie draws a glass of water to
                    her lips but suddenly stops.

MILLIE
Is that the same bayonet that was taken from the cabinet?

                    Alf slowly nods.

>   Bev suddenly stands and opens
>   her bag and places the bayonet
>   on the table.
>
>   They are open-jawed.
>
>   Alf is shocked.

ALF
You of all people?

MILLIE
You of all people?

BEV
Yes, me of all people. Sorry Alf. Was meant to be a joke. Would have never taken it knowing the story behind it.

MORRIS
Why did you take it, luv?

BEV
Oh I dunno. I guess I'm sick of that cabinet. And that flag. That bloody flag! It's like the bloody shroud of Turin. (sighs) I'm sorry, Alf.

>   Rosemary picks up the photo
>   album.

ROSEMARY
These photos in the back here . Where we these taken?

ALF
Darwin. We were stationed there before we were shipped out. Some of the photos are colour but they are only hand painted.

MORRIS
They did that then. The local chemist boy would paint your photos with a tiny brush.

> Kevin returns looking stoned. He passes Bev a joint which she slips in her handbag.

ROSEMARY
But what about these photos? These photos of Aboriginal women brawling on the dirt. You're all standing around laughing at them.

ALF
Yes, a bit of cat fight, that.

ROSEMARY
Cat fight!?

MILLIE
Didn't any of you try and stop it?

ALF
Nothing to do with us.

ROSEMARY
(jumps to her feet)
So your entertainment was to watch two Aboriginal women kicking the life out of each other in the dirt as you stand around laughing?

> Alf shrugs.

BEV
(dryly)
I want my curling iron back?

> We suddenly hear an announcement of the intercom.

BRIAN (V.O.)
Attention patrons...

> A plastic torch/effigy lights up in the corner of the stage.

BRIAN (V.O.)
Will you please be upstanding for the ode.

> The quartet of soldiers obediently turn and face west.
>
> Rosemary remains seated.

BRIAN (V.O.)
"They shall grow not old, as we that are left grow old;
Age shall not weary them, nor the years condemn.
At the going down of the sun and in the morning
We will remember them. Lest we forget."

CAST
Lest we forget...

> We hear the Last Post.

BRIAN (V.O.)
Thank you patrons.

> Lights out.
>
> Cast exits the stage.

ACT 2 SCENE 1

> Following week. The day before ANZAC Day.
>
> Lights are raised. The stage has been transformed into a boardroom. We see a long table, a white-board with sales hype scrawled over it, an Australian flag and a portrait of a young Queen Elizabeth in the corner, stage-left.
>
> The quartet of soldiers enter and sit at the board table (finally).
>
> Bev enters with a plate of party pies.

BEV
Brian said he's pleased yous are finally back in the boardroom and to thank yous for your patience and to have a plate of complimentary pies on the club.

ALF
More bloody pies? Why have you called this emergency meeting tonight, Morris?

MORRIS
Before we march tomorrow, the ladies are coming over this evening to talk about their war.

ALF
What do you bloody mean, "their war?" (sotto voce) Strike me pink!

MORRIS
They feel we've shared our experiences with them. Now it's their turn to talk about women in war.

ALF
What would they know about bloody war? (sotto voce) Strike me pink!

PERCY
(shrugs)
We'll find out, no doubt.

MORRIS
They feel they need to explain why they need to march with us. (pulls out an old fob watch) I hope they arrive soon. I'm meeting Ivy for tea at Sizzler.

PERCY
Yes, it's the dawn service tomorrow. I need an early night.

ALF
This is bloody ridiculous! They won't be marching, period. The law has put a stop to that, remember? Nothing will change my mind on the matter.

PERCY
They know that. But we need to hear them out, Alf. Fair's fair.

> Rosemary and a very pregnant Millie enter. Rosemary clutches a briefcase.

> There is a moody silence.

ROSEMARY
Good evening gentlemen. You've told us about your war. Showed us pictures. Shared anecdotes. Before the march tomorrow, we need to tell you about ours.

ALF
What bloody war? What are you rabbiting on about?

ROSEMARY
Women in war.

> Rosemary throws 10x8 black and white photos on the boardroom table along with some papers.

ROSEMARY
When the Japanese invaded the British colony of Hong Kong in December, 1941, over ten thousand Chinese women were raped or gang-raped by the Japanese soldiers. These are some of the official reports. Pretty grizzly stuff.

> The men study the reports, distressed.

ALF
(reading, shaking his head)
Animals the lot of them!

PERCY
(reading)
I had heard about the Japanese in Hong Kong.

MORRIS
(reading)
Like I said, the Japs were very mean in the war.

> Millie hands around more photos.

ROSEMARY
Not just the Japanese. Upwards of two million German women were raped in 1945 in a tidal wave of looting, burning and vengeance by the Allies.

ALF
Russians. Not Allies.

PERCY
They were wild with rage in Berlin, I'm told.

ROSEMARY
Moscow encouraged its troops to regard German women as targets for revenge.

> Millie hands out photos and reports.

BEV
(reading, quite disturbed)
Bloody Russians. I need vodka.

> Bev hits the bar.

ROSEMARY
(reading)
Russian Marshal Georgi Zhukov called on his troops to - and I quote - "Remember our brothers and sisters, our mothers and

fathers, our wives and children tortured to death by Germans....We shall exact a brutal revenge for everything."

MILLIE
The subtext was 'rape as many German women as possible'.

ROSEMARY
Another example of rape used as a weapon of war.

PERCY
The Germans brutalised the Russians during the war. And the Czechs. And the Poles. In fact, we had a couple of Polish boys flying with us. When no one in their right mind would go up, they would take off in Spits in pea-soupers to attack 109s. The Poles were crazed with revenge.

MILLIE
It gets worse. Chinese scholars say some 410,000 women were forced into 'comfort stations'. In other words, forced to become prostitutes.

ALF
They were very cruel to the Chinese and Korean girls. I know. We liberated some of them in Java.

ROSEMARY
This included 300 Dutch women from across the Dutch East Indies.

ALF
I remember that, too.

MILLIE
Approximately three quarters of all comfort women died, and most survivors were left infertile due to sexual trauma or

sexually transmitted disease.

ROSEMARY
According to one Japanese soldier, Yasuji Kaneko, "The women cried out, but it didn't matter to us whether the women lived or died. We were the emperor's soldiers. Whether in military brothels or in the villages, we raped without reluctance."

>Alf slams his walking stick on the table.

ALF
But don't you see, Millie? This is what we were fighting against. These people would have brutalised even more women and enslaved half the world, if we didn't stop them. This is what we are trying to tell you! (sotto voce) For the love of Mike!

MILLIE
I agree. But why can't we remember these women, too, Pop? It was their war as much as your war. Why can't they be represented? I simply don't understand what the problem is.

BEV
(quietly to Rosemary)
You know why.

KEVIN
(nodding)
Too dark.

BEV
(nodding)
Too dark.

MILLIE
But don't you see that by not acknowledging it, Pop, you allow it to keep happening.

ALF
I allow it? *Me*? What have I got to bloody do with it?

BEV
What she's saying, Alf, is that you allow it by stopping the girls from marching.

> Alf slams his walking-stick on the table.

ALF
This is *not your war*!

> Rosemary gets to her feet

ROSEMARY
Don't you see? This is our war. Because our war never ends. Women fight these battles every day.

ALF
Rubbish.

ROSEMARY
You've shared your war. Now let me tell you about my war, Mr Watson.

> Alf tuts.

ROSEMARY
My journey to hell and back began twelve years ago. When I met my husband Tony-

ALF/MORRIS/PERCY/KEV/BEV
Husband!?

ROSEMARY
(glaring)
Husband.

> Rosemary is picked up by a spotlight.

ROSEMARY
I met Tony when he moved next door. He was an ex-Vietnam vet.

KEVIN
I like him already.

ROSEMARY
That may change when you hear my story. We became friends and later he moved in with me and we became an item. He had me hook, line and sinker. A real charmer. We married that year. His old regiment formed a guard of honour on the day. Quite romantic.

One night we were out with some of his old army buddies. He'd been drinking all day and I was upset so I sat in the car. He came bellowing over so I quickly locked the door. Then he put his fist right through the passenger window and dragged me through it. After receiving a punch in the head, one of his ex-army mates drove me to the hospital. He told me a lot about Tony in Vietnam that Tony never told *me*. Dark things. At hospital they tended to my injuries, cuts and bruises but what hurt most was that it happened at all. It just...came out of nowhere. The next day when he arrived at the flat he was full of remorse - things would be different, he said. He wouldn't drink and he would never hurt me again.

I believed him [sighs] and things improved for a while. They really did. Soon I discovered I was pregnant. He seemed over the moon with the news. A few months later he came home drunk, and after arguing he punched me in the stomach. I ended up in hospital with a ruptured cyst on my ovary.

PERCY
The beast!

ROSEMARY
The baby was all right but I wasn't. Returning home I gave him an ultimatum - the booze or me. He chose me.

However, after our baby was born the demons returned. The drinking returned, and the abuse continued. I stayed, as I couldn't see a way out. Brief times when he was sober, things were fine. But soon my life became moving from one house to another with him, as people became aware of the domestic violence - although I had learned to hide the bruises and he became very good at not leaving them where they could be seen. Over the years I took out several Intervention Orders, which I then dropped when he made his promises and sometimes, even, threats against me.

I got pregnant again, this time with twins. When I was pregnant we moved again, this time to be closer to his family, as I was going to need help and support with twins on the way. This was a bad move. You see, his father - who'd fought in WW2 - also had a drinking problem. They were a bad influence on each other.

BEV
The apple never falls far from the tree.

ROSEMARY
You got that right. So during my pregnancy he abused me again and again. There were times when he was at the pub with his dad, I would pray that someone would knock on my door and tell me he was dead, rather than face him coming home. I was trapped. The only people I knew were his family. I had no way out.

Once our new babies were born, things remained the same. I looked after the children. He went to the pub or to smoke dope with an ex-army mate. Life was tough and often there was no money for food. I stopped eating so what we had would go further. As long as he had his booze he didn't care. He would complain when the babies cried and tell me 'to shut them up or else.' Every day I lived in fear, never knowing what his mood would be. I was not only frightened for myself but for the children.

I found the phone book and looked under 'Domestic Violence'. The first few refuges were full and asked if I could wait. Can you believe it? A waiting list!? Finally I rang a Salvation Army refuge, and an elderly man answered; I don't know how he understood me through my sobs as I tried to tell my story. He said 'grab some things. I'm on my way to pick you up right now.' Well, I grabbed my photo albums, a garbage bag of clothes for the children and myself and threw everything into his car and he floored it. You've never seen a pensioner drive so fast.

They all laugh

MORRIS
Good old Salvos! Is that why you put $20 in the box before?

ROSEMARY
(shrugs, nods)

Figure I owe them. Anyway, waking up in the refuge that morning, I was a scared of the future, but not like I had been every day for the last five years. The eggshells I had been treading on were gone, my children could cry and I didn't have to feel sick with fear. I was determined to turn my life around.

I spent a week at that refuge before moving interstate. Changed my name. Began to rebuild my life. A few months later, I moved into a housing commission house, got part time work, and had started making friends for the first time since leaving school. Life was just great.

Till he found me again. Fourteen months later, after I trusted the wrong person, he contacted me. He pleaded with me to believe that he had changed, he'd been to counselling, anger management, all provided by the veterans association and Legacy etc. He was convincing - the old charm was back. I agreed to give it a trial, but said that things would have to go slowly. He couldn't live with me. And no more alcohol. He saw us once a month to begin with as he lived a long way away. Soon he moved to the town where I was living.

One weekend he was staying with us, he started drinking. We argued and I asked him to leave, he refused. I went to phone the police. He hit the phone out of my hands and pushed me to my knees. He put one hand around my throat and squeezed. I was able to break away and I ran out the front door. He caught up to me in the neighbour's garden, pushed me to the ground and started punching and kicking me. I thought he was going to kill me. A female voice called out that she had called the police and he fled. I believe if it wasn't for the intervention of a stranger, I'd not be here today. When the kids were old enough I decided to educate myself. Put myself through uni. I cleaned toilets at night. Made it all work somehow. Here I am to tell the tale.

ALF
I'm sorry for you Mz Smith. I really am. Your husband was a bloody disgrace. And a disgrace to the uniform. I'll admit that. But nothing will make me change my mind. ANZAC Day is our day. Not yours.

ROSEMARY
Millie, it's time for you to tell your story.

>   Millie shakes her head furtively at Rosemary.

MILLIE
No.

ROSEMARY
We have no choice.

MILLIE
Rosemary we agreed it was only–

ALF
Tell me what?

>   Millie sighs and sits down.

MILLIE
I was raped, Pop.

>   Alf is open-mouthed.

ALF
Tell me it's not true, sweetheart.

MILLIE
It's true, Pop.

ALF
(pointing to Millie's belly)
So this is not my grandchild?

MILLIE
(smiling)
Only the good half.

ALF
Does Mark know?

MILLIE
Yes, my husband's supporting me through it; whatever happens. That's if I live through the labour. As you now I have pre-eclampsia.

ALF
(quietly)
Yes Peggy told me. It will be touch and go, she said. So tell me what happened. (soto voce) I can't believe this is happening.

> Millie pours some water and steadies herself.

MILLIE
It was last New Year's Eve. I was walking past a fire station on my way to meet friends to see the fireworks at The Rocks when I was grabbed by a fireman, dragged into the station house and raped. He thought I should be happy about it. Pleased. New Year's Eve and everything. But I was sobbing. So he threw my dress at me which he'd ripped off my back and said if I was to go to the police he'd say it was consensual. I went to the police

regardless. But he was right. They all knew each other. Closed ranks. Said they didn't have enough to prosecute in the end.

There was no evidence because I'd had a shower to wash his rotten filth off me. But it got better. (Patting her belly) He made me pregnant.

I went for an abortion six months ago and was spat on by right-to-lifers outside a clinic in Darlinghurst. So I ran away and never went through with it.

> Alf throws his stick across the room.

ALF
Fucking bastards!

> Millie is shocked. She returns his stick.

MILLIE
That's the first time I've heard you really swear, Pop.

ALF
Can you blame me, pet?

> There is a reflective pause here.
>
> Rosemary shrugs and mouths an apology to Millie. Millie hangs her head.

ROSEMARY
Mr Watson, last time we were here, in order to underscore your argument and dissuade us from attempting to join the march,

you showed us graphic photos of your war.

> Rosemary walks around the table and places photos in front of them.

ROSEMARY
These are our war photos. Inside this manila envelope are photos and medical reports of a young nurse who was gang-raped, and murdered. I obtained these through a source in the police force sympathetic to the plight of women. The public will never see these photos. Steady yourselves gentlemen.

> They read the reports and study the photos. From the looks on their faces we see they are shocking images.

MORRIS
This poor nurse. Where was she stationed?

ROSEMARY
Blacktown?

KEVIN
Blacktown? I don't understand.

PERCY
What was this poor lass's name?

ROSEMARY
Anita Coby.

> Everyone is visually upset.

Morris stands and walks over to the portrait of the young Queen Elizabeth and turns it so it faces the wall.

Lights out.

We hear a long BLOOD CURDLING SCREAM in the darkness.

EPILOGUE

Lights are raised. The stage is set back to an RSL club lounge. We hear a faint soundtrack of the pokies with their tedious, sour unending melodies.

Alf, Percy, Morris, Kevin are sitting around a table of beers. They drink in rueful silence.

Rosemary enters wearing a white ribbon. She passes Alf flowers. She exits. Alf is stoic but visibly upset.

Morris and Percy pats Alf on the shoulder in sympathy.

We suddenly hear an announcement of the intercom.

BRIAN (V.O.)
Attention patrons...

> A plastic torch/effigy lights in the corner of the stage.

BRIAN (V.O.)
Will you please be upstanding for the ode.

> The quartet of soldiers obediently stand, turn and face west.

BRIAN (V.O.)
"They shall grow not old, as we that are left grow old;
Age shall not weary them, nor the years condemn.
At the going down of the sun and in the morning
We will remember them. Lest we forget."

> We hear the Last Post.
>
> The veterans - as they do each night at the club - obediently face west.
>
> However, as the Last Post shrouds the room in memory, Percy reaches into his pocket and pins the white ribbon to his breast.
>
> The others slowly follow.
>
> Alf is last to pin the white ribbon to his jacket.

Stage lights fade.

Blackout

OTHER TITLES AVAILABLE FROM
ORiGiN™ THEATRICAL

FEEDEM FIGHTERS
Dorian Mode

Daryl Lucas is a fat, happily married soft-drink salesman living on the NSW Central Coast until the day he walks in on his cheating cougar wife and her young Pilates instructor. While he plots to divorce her, she arranges for Daryl to be kidnapped by a group of disparate lunatics calling themselves Feedem Fighters. Inspired by shows like Extreme Makeover and The Biggest Loser, these calorie terrorists kidnap fatties and keep them captive in a soundproof room for three months, forcing them to lose weight. Can Daryl convince them he's only being held so his wife can drain his accounts and run off with her Pilates instructor?

Feedem Fighters is a seemingly innocuous comedy but below the waistline it canvasses issues and themes that touch the public's collective soul in the perplexing duality of this image-obsessed / food-obsessed society we now find ourselves in...

"You'll laugh so much you'll lose two kilos!"

Cast: 5 Male & 1 Female
Full Length Play, Australian, Comedy, Present Day

www.origintheatrical.com.au

OTHER TITLES AVAILABLE FROM ORiGiN™ THEATRICAL

CONNECTED
Craig Christie

CONNECTED explores the dangers and consequences of the interface between life and the online world in a story that resonates throughout schools and households everywhere.

Emma arrives at a new school and runs the gauntlet of finding out about friendship groups and how the game is played in this new setting. Meanwhile Dylan's social awkwardness means he is spending more and more time on his computer locked away in his room. When Emma finds herself the object of unwanted attention of the school jock Michael, his ex girlfriend Kate uses any means available to put the new girl in her place. The entire situation takes a turn towards the sinister as their online worlds collides with their lives in a way over which they ultimately have no control and which threatens to have the most disastrous consequences.

"The pace was fast moving and we witnessed the rapid snowballing effect born from the use of modern technology mixed with tricks, lies and deceit. 'Connected' is a perfect platform for young actors to perform to their utmost strengths, the work is vocally demanding and offers the best of opportunities for great acting.
– Scott Jarrett. Whakatane, New Zealand

Cast: 2 Male & 2 Female
Full Length Musical, Australian, Drama, 21st Century

www.origintheatrical.com.au

Printed by Libri Plureos GmbH in Hamburg, Germany